New York City Buildings

by Ann Mace

photos by Tim Holmstrom

 Richard C. Owen Publishers, Inc.
Katonah, New York

New York City is full of buildings.

This building is famous.

This building is round.

This building is narrow.

These buildings are very, very tall.

This building is beautiful.
It shines in the daylight.

It shines at night.

This building is guarded by lions.

But the best building in New York City
is this building . . .

because we live there!